Walt Disney
PICTURES PRESENTS

THE Tigger MOVIE

Family of Tiggers

Victoria Saxon • Illustrated by Josie Yee

DISNEY PRESS

New York

Afternoon sunlight lit up the Hundred-Acre Wood when Owl invited Tigger and Roo for tea.

"Hoo-hoo-*HOO!*" cheered Tigger. "You betcha, Beak Lips, me and Roo'd love some snappy snacks and drinkedy-drinks!"

"Did I ever tell you the story
of how my family first began?"
asked Owl.

As Owl began to tell Tigger and Roo the story

of his family tree, starting from its deepest roots,

Tigger's imagination started to bounce around.

A family fulla tiggers, thought Tigger.

Now that would be somethin' ta

talk about. . . .

"This story goes back a long, long time," Owl went on.

Say, a long, long time ago, thought Tigger, why, I betcha my family had saber-toof tiggers way back there somewhere and a great big tiggersaurus, too. *R-rr-rowwr-r!*

"And that brings us up to my great-great-grandmother and my great-great-grandfather," droned Owl. "One day on a morning ride . . ."

Hoo-hoo-*hooo!* thought Tigger. My great-great-grandtigger was probably all fulla vim an' vigor ridin' along in his little ol-fashionedy car.

I can just see it now, thought Tigger. Great-great-grandmomma Tigger sped right past 'im! He was bein' all debonairy, while she was speedin' up an' finishin' up firstest!

Oh, I'm sure and certain my
tigger family was terrifically famous for
having the most pounce to the ounce!

There was a whole buncha athletical
tiggers that won great big sporty events like
the fifty-yard bounce and the relay pounce.

And there was a great whole big buncha
gymnastickal tiggers, too.

And hula-hoopin' tiggers,

and ticklish tiggers
that loved to giggle.
Hoo-hoo-ha!

There were adventuresome tiggers, like mountain
bouncers and deep-sea pouncers. And brave captain
tiggers that sailed the several seas.

And the chef tiggers cooked up the most splendiferous sandywiches—on account of their secret ingredient being real sand, o' course.

And those poetickal tiggers were smart and intelligentickal. Maybe they were the first-ever inventors of the doohickey, the thingamabob, and the whatchamacallit!

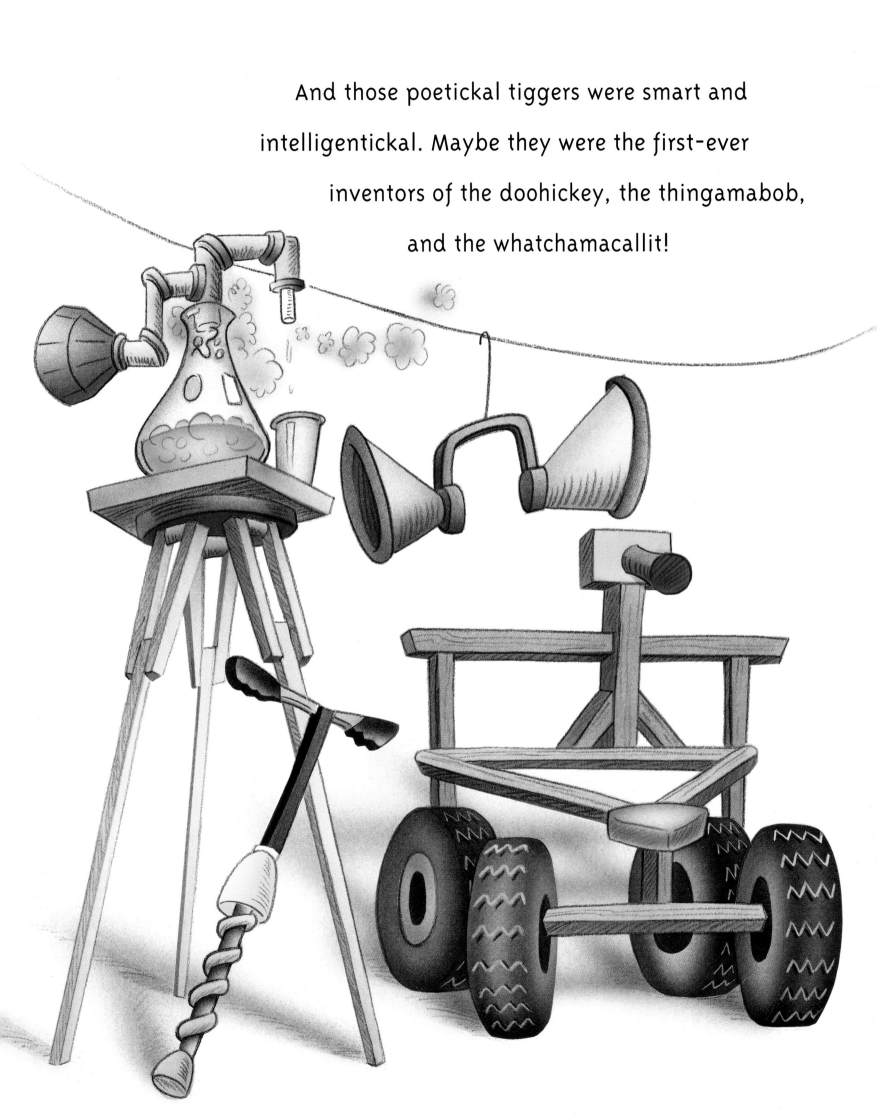

And even up in the stars, there were asternaut
tiggers and oogly-boogly green Martian tiggers!

They scooted those
stars into the shape of
the Big Tigger
and the Little Tigger.

And when I think of those smarty-pants
tiggers—hoo-hoo—they were champion
spellers: T-I—double Guh—Rrr spells Tigger!

And o' course a tigger never brags, but when it comes
to snapping a snazzy shot, we tiggers have always been
a more 'n fairly photogenical lot.

"Harrrumph!" said Owl rather loudly. Tigger

jumped up and saw Owl and Roo staring at him.

"You seem to have slipped into a state

of unconscionable unawakeness."

"You were snoring, Tigger,"
Roo whispered to his pal.

Oh, well, Tigger thought. I may have been dreaming about my family fulla tiggers, but what an absoposilutely wunnerful buncha fellas and fellerettes they were! Hoo-hoo-*HOOOOO!*

for Louise and Glenn — V. S.

for my parents, my husband, and my daughter Ana, — J. Y.